P9-CCF-660

•Abenteuer mit Nikolaus•

Die verschwundene Katze

•Adventures with Nicholas•

The Missing Cat

Illustrated by
Chris L. Demarest

Berlitz Kids™
Berlitz Publishing Company, Inc.

Princeton, New Jersey   Mexico City, Mexico   Dublin, Ireland
Eschborn, Germany   Singapore, Singapore

Copyright © 1996 by Berlitz Publishing Company, Inc.
Berlitz Kids™
400 Alexander Park
Princeton, NJ 08540

Berlitz Kids is a trademark of, and the Berlitz name and logotype
are registered trademarks of, Berlitz Investment Corporation.

All rights reserved. No part of this book (or accompanying recordings)
may be reproduced or transmitted in any form or by any means, electronic
or mechanical, including photocopying, recording or by any information
storage and retrieval system, without permission from the Publisher.

Printed in USA

1   3   5   7   9   10   8   6   4   2

ISBN 2-8315-5743-7

Dear Parents,

One of the most enriching experiences a child can have is learning a new language. Young children love learning, and Berlitz makes learning a new language more fun than ever before.

In 1878, Professor Maximilian Berlitz had a revolutionary idea about making language learning accessible and enjoyable. These same principles are still successfully at work today. Developed by an experienced team of language experts and educators, Berlitz Kids products are based on our century-old commitment to excellence as well as on the latest research about teaching children a second language.

One of the great joys of parenting is learning and discovering by listening to stories with your child. This is the very best way for a child to acquire beginning knowledge of a second language. In fact, by about the age of four, many children enjoy hearing stories for as long as 15 minutes.

The materials you are holding in your hands—*Adventures with Nicholas*—are designed to introduce children to a second language in a positive, accessible, and enjoyable way. The eight episodes present foreign language words gradually. And the content and vocabulary have been carefully chosen to interest and involve your child. You can use the materials at home, of course. You can also use them in the car, on the bus, or anywhere at all.

On one side of the audio cassette your child will hear the stories with wonderful sound effects. On the other side, your child will sing along with the entertaining and memorable songs. The songs are not just fun. Language experts say that singing songs helps kids learn the sounds of a new language more easily. What's more, an audio dictionary helps your child learn pronunciations of important words.

As you listen to the stories, be sure to take your cues from your child. Above all, keep it fun.

Welcome!

The Editors at Berlitz Kids

1 Wo ist Prinzessin?

Where Is Princess?

Nikolaus liebt seine Katze.
Sie heißt Prinzessin.

Nicholas loves his cat.
Her name is Princess.

„O nein!
Wo ist Prinzessin?"

"Oh, no!
Where is Princess?"

Hans ist der Bruder von Nikolaus.
„Hallo, Hans! Wo ist Prinzessin?"
„Das weiß ich nicht."

John is Nicholas's brother.
"Hi, John, where is Princess?"
"I don't know."

„Guten Morgen, Mutti! Wo ist Prinzessin?"
„Das weiß ich nicht."

"Good morning, Mom. Where is Princess?"
"I don't know."

Maria ist die Schwester von Nikolaus.
„Hallo, Maria! Wo ist Prinzessin?"
„Das weiß ich nicht."

Maria is Nicholas's sister.
"Hi, Maria, where is Princess?"
"I don't know."

„Guten Morgen, Vati! Wo ist Prinzessin?"
     fragt Nikolaus.
„Das weiß ich nicht. Gehen wir sie doch suchen,"
     sagt sein Vati.
„Ich will mitgehen," sagt Maria.
Also gehen Nikolaus, Maria und ihr Vati Prinzessin
     suchen.

"Good morning, Dad. Where is Princess?" asks Nicholas.
"I don't know. Let's go look for her," says his dad.
"I want to go, too," says Maria.
So, Nicholas, Maria, and their dad go out to look for Princess.

Die Suche nach Prinzessin

Looking for Princess

Nikolaus, Maria und ihr Vati suchen Prinzessin.
„Prinzessin, wo bist du?"
„Prinzessin, wo bist du?"
„Prinzessin, wo bist du?"

Nicholas, Maria, and their dad are looking for Princess.
"Princess, where are you?"
"Princess, where are you?"
"Princess, where are you?"

Sie suchen hier.

They look here.

Sie suchen da.

They look there.

Sie suchen überall.

They look everywhere.

Nikolaus sieht Prinzessin nicht.
Aber er sieht Essen!
„Ich habe Hunger," sagt Nikolaus.
„Ich habe Durst," sagt sein Vati.
„Ich habe Hunger und Durst," sagt Maria.

Nicholas doesn't see Princess.
But he does see food!
"I'm hungry," says Nicholas.
"I'm thirsty," says his dad.
"I'm hungry and thirsty," says Maria.

„Willst du einen Apfel?"
„Nein! Ich will keinen Apfel," sagt Nikolaus.
„Willst du Trauben?"
„Nein! Ich will keine Trauben."

"Do you want an apple?"
"No. I don't want an apple," says Nicholas.
"Do you want some grapes?"
"No. I don't want some grapes."

„Was willst du denn?"
„Ich will eine Banane!" sagt Nikolaus.
„Mmm! Ist die gut! Danke schön, Vati!"
„Bitte schön, Nikolaus!"

"What do you want?"
"I want a banana!" says Nicholas.
"Mmm! That's good. Thanks, Dad!"
"You're welcome, Nicholas!"

„Guten Tag! Ich suche meine Katze.
Sie heißt Prinzessin.
Wissen Sie, wo sie ist?"

*"Hello. I'm looking for my cat.
Her name is Princess.
Do you know where she is?"*

„Vielleicht ist sie da drüben."
„Vati, suchen wir doch da drüben," sagt Nikolaus.
„Eine gute Idee," sagen sein Vati und Maria.
Und sie ziehen los.

*"Maybe she's over there."
"Dad, let's look over there," says Nicholas.
"Good idea," say his dad and Maria.
And away they go.*

3 Das Bild von Prinzessin

Princess's Picture

„Komm schon, Nikolaus,
   holen wir uns Hilfe!"
„Meine Katze ist verschwunden,"
   sagt Nikolaus.
„Können Sie mir bitte helfen?"

"Come on, Nicholas.
Let's get help."
"My cat is lost," says Nicholas.
"Can you please help me?"

„Na klar! Ich kann dir helfen.
Ist deine Katze groß oder klein, Nikolaus?"
„Sie ist klein," sagt Nikolaus.

"Sure, I can help you.
Is your cat big or little, Nicholas?"
"She's little," says Nicholas.

„Ist sie weiß?"
„Nein, sie ist nicht weiß."

"Is she white?"
"No. She isn't white."

„Ist sie schwarz?"
„Nein, sie ist nicht
schwarz."

"Is she black?"
"No. She isn't black."

20

„Ist sie rosa?"
„Nein, nein! Sie ist nicht rosa!
Prinzessin ist orange."

"Is she pink?"
"No, no! She isn't pink!
Princess is orange."

„Ja! Das ist Prinzessin. Danke schön!"
„Bitte schön! Komm mit, hängen wir
     diese Bilder überall in der
     Stadt auf."
Und das tun sie.

"Yes, that's Princess! Thank you!"
"You're welcome. Let's put these pictures
     all around the town."
And that's what they do.

Zehn Prinzessinnen

Ten Princesses

„Gehen wir doch zur
  Bücherei, Vati.
Eine Menge Leute gehen
  zur Bücherei."

*"Let's go to the library, Dad.
Lots of people go to the library."*

„Gehen wir doch zum Postamt," sagt der Vati
    von Nikolaus.
„Eine Menge Leute gehen zum Postamt."
„Das stimmt," sagt Maria.

"Let's go to the post office," says Nicholas's dad.
"Lots of people go to the post office."
"That's right," says Maria.

„Gehen wir doch zum Hotel.
Eine Menge Leute gehen
zum Hotel."

*"Let's go to the hotel.
Lots of people go to the hotel."*

„Gehen wir doch zum Lebensmittelladen
   und zur Bäckerei.
Eine Menge Leute gehen auch dahin."

*"Let's go to the grocery store and the bakery.
Lots of people go there, too."*

Sie gehen überall in der Stadt herum.
„Vielen Dank für Ihre Hilfe," sagt Nikolaus.
„Danke schön!" sagt Maria.
„Bitte schön!"

They go all around the town.
"Thank you for helping," says Nicholas.
"Thank you very much!" says Maria.
"You're welcome!"

Nikolaus zählt.
„Eins, zwei, drei, vier, fünf,
    sechs, sieben, acht, neun, zehn.
Zehn Bilder von Prinzessin!"
Nikolaus und Maria fühlen sich schon besser.

Nicholas counts.
"One, two, three, four, five,
    six, seven, eight, nine, ten.
Ten pictures of Princess!"
Nicholas and Maria feel better already.

5 Bei der Feuerwehr

At the Firehouse

„Wir haben noch ein Bild.
Bringen wir das doch zur Feuerwehr,"
    sagt Nikolaus.

*"We have one more picture.
Let's take it to the firehouse," says Nicholas.*

„Guten Tag. Können Sie uns helfen?" fragt Nikolaus.
„Brennt es?"
„Nein. Ich suche meine Katze."
„Brennt deine Katze?"
„Nein, sie ist verschwunden."
„Sie sieht so aus," sagt der Vati von Nikolaus.

"Hello. Can you help us?" asks Nicholas.
"Is there a fire?"
"No. I'm looking for my cat."
"Is your cat on fire?"
"No, she's lost."
"She looks like this," says Nicholas's dad.

„Hmmm. Laßt mal sehen:
Am Sonntag keine Katze.
Am Montag keine Katze.

"Hmmm. Let me see.
On Sunday, no cat.
On Monday, no cat.

Am Dienstag keine Katze.
Am Mittwoch keine Katze.
Am Donnerstag keine Katze.
Am Freitag keine Katze."

On Tuesday, no cat.
On Wednesday, no cat.
On Thursday, no cat.
On Friday, no cat."

32

„Heute ist Samstag.
Keine Katze heute.
Keine Katze die ganze Woche.
Tut mir leid. Ich kann euch nicht helfen.
Aber ruft mich, wenn ihr ein Feuer seht."

"Today is Saturday.
No cat today.
No cat all week.
I'm sorry. I can't help you.
But call me if you see a fire."

„Niemand kann Prinzessin finden," sagt Nikolaus.
„Prinzessin ist immer noch verschwunden."
„Gib nicht auf!" sagt sein Vati.
„Gib nicht auf!" sagt seine Schwester.
Nikolaus lächelt.
Aber er denkt „Prinzessin fehlt mir trotzdem."

"No one can find Princess," says Nicholas.
"Princess is still lost."
"Don't give up," says his dad.
"Don't give up," says his sister.
Nicholas smiles.
But he thinks, "I still miss Princess."

6 Erinnerungen an Prinzessin

Remembering Princess

Nikolaus erinnert sich an seine Katze.
„Im Frühling mag Prinzessin die Blumen.
Sie spielt im Garten."

Nicholas remembers his cat.
"In the spring, Princess likes the flowers.
She plays in the garden."

„Im Sommer mag Prinzessin die Fische.
Sie spielt am Teich.
Aber sie macht sich nicht gern naß!"

"In the summer, Princess likes the fish.
She plays by the pond.
But she doesn't like to get wet!"

„Im Herbst mag sie die Blätter.
Sie spielt in den Bäumen."

"In the fall, she likes the leaves.
She plays in the trees."

„Im Winter mag Prinzessin den Schnee.
Sie spielt mit mir."

"In the winter, Princess likes the snow.
She plays with me."

„Schaut mal, wer da kommt!
Und schaut mal, was er trägt!
Guten Tag! Ist Prinzessin da drin?" fragt Nikolaus.
„Nein, Nikolaus, leider nicht.
Es ist nicht Prinzessin."

"Look who's coming!
And look what he's carrying!
Hello. Is Princess in there?" asks Nicholas.
"No, Nicholas, I'm sorry.
It's not Princess."

Aber eine Katze habe ich doch.
Sie ist sehr niedlich,
   und sie braucht ein Heim.
Könnt ihr sie zu euch nehmen?"
„Ja, ja!" sagt Nikolaus.
Und so bekommt Nikolaus
   seinen neuen Kater.

"But I do have a cat.
He's very cute,
   and he needs a home.
Can you take him in?"
"Yes, yes," says Nicholas.
And that is how Nicholas gets
   his new cat.

7 Eine Katze, Zwei Katzen

One Cat, Two Cats

Nikolaus ruft seine Mutti.
„Mutti! Schau mal!
Wir haben ein neues Kätzchen."
„Toll!" sagt Mutti.
Nikolaus ruft seinen Bruder.
„Hans! Schau mal!
Wir haben ein neues Kätzchen."
„Toll!" sagt Hans.

Nicholas calls his mom.
"Mom! Look!
We have a new kitten."
"Great!" says Mom.
Nicholas calls his brother.
"John! Look!
We have a new kitten."
"Great!" says John.

Das Kätzchen schaut sich
    überall im Haus um.
Es spielt in der Küche.
Es läuft herum und herum.
Es findet Futter.
„Es mag es!" sagt Nikolaus.

The kitten looks all around the house.
He plays in the kitchen.
He runs around and around.
He finds some food.
"He likes it," says Nicholas.

Das Kätzchen spielt im Wohnzimmer.
Es findet sein Bett.
„Es mag es!" sagt Nikolaus.

The kitten plays in the living room.
He finds his bed.
"He likes it," says Nicholas.

Das Kätzchen spielt im Badezimmer.
Es läuft rauf und runter.
Es findet eine Spielzeugmaus.
„Es mag sie! Es mag sie sehr!"

The kitten plays in the bathroom.
He runs up and down.
He finds a toy mouse.
"He likes it. He likes it a lot."

Das Kätzchen spielt im Schlafzimmer.
Es läuft herum und herum,
   rein und raus,
   und rauf und runter.
Schaut mal, was es findet!

The kitten plays in the bedroom.
He runs around and around,
   in and out,
   and up and down.
Look what he finds!

Prinzessin!
„Prinzessin, ich liebe dich!" sagt Nikolaus.
„Ich liebe dich auch!" sagt Maria.
„Ich liebe dich auch!" sagt Hans.

Princess!
"Princess, I love you," says Nicholas.
"I love you, too," says Maria.
"I love you, too," says John.

„Schau mal, Mutti! Schau mal, Vati!
Prinzessin ist da!"
Prinzessin mag das Kätzchen.
Das Kätzchen mag Prinzessin auch.
Und Nikolaus ist sehr, sehr glücklich.

"Look, Mom! Look, Dad!
It's Princess!"
Princess likes the kitten.
The kitten likes Princess, too.
And Nicholas feels very, very happy.

8 Die Party

The Party

„Jetzt haben wir zwei Katzen," sagt Nikolaus.
„Feiern wir das!"
„Ja!" sagt Mutti. „Machen wir doch um sieben
   Uhr eine Party!"

"Now we have two cats," says Nicholas.
"Let's celebrate!"
"Yes!" says Mom. "Let's have a party at seven o'clock."

„Vati, kann wir die Party jetzt anfangen?"
   fragt Nikolaus.
„Nein, Nikolaus, es ist erst fünf Uhr.
Die Party fängt in zwei Stunden an."

"Dad, can we start the party now?" asks Nicholas.
"No, Nicholas, it's only five o'clock.
The party starts in two hours."

„Maria, kann die Party jetzt anfangen?"
„Nein, Nikolaus, es ist erst sechs Uhr.
Die Party fängt in einer Stunde an."

"Maria, can we start the party now?"
"No, Nicholas, it's only six o'clock.
The party starts in one hour."

„Hurra! Es ist sieben Uhr.
Es ist Zeit für die Party!" sagt Nikolaus.

"Hooray! It's seven o'clock.
It's time for the party!" says Nicholas.

„Darf ich ein Eis haben?" fragt Nikolaus.
„Ich auch?" fragt Hans.
„Ja!" sagt die Mutti.
„Darf ich Kuchen haben?" fragt Nikolaus.
„Ich auch?" fragt Hans.
„Ja!" sagt die Mutti.

"May I have some ice cream?" asks Nicholas
"Me too?" asks John.
"Yes," says Mom.
"May I have some cake?" asks Nicholas.
"Me too?" asks John.
"Yes," says Mom.

„Was für eine tolle Party!" sagt Maria.
„Wir haben so viel Glück!" sagt Nikolaus.
„Wir sind eine große, glückliche Familie!"

"What a great party!" says Maria.
"We're so lucky!" says Nicholas.
"We're one big, happy family!"

Song Lyrics

Song to Accompany Story 1

Miau! *(Meow!)*

[Sung to the tune of "Oh Where, Oh Where Has My Little Dog Gone?"]

O wohin, wohin,
Ist meine Katze gelaufen?
O wo, o wo kann sie sein?
Mit Ohren so kurz,
Und ihrem Schwanz so lang,
Ich glaube, sie ist auf dem Baum!
MIAU!

O wohin, wohin,
Ist meine Katze gelaufen?
O wo, o wo kann sie sein?
Mit Ohren so kurz,
Und ihrem Schwanz so lang,
Ich glaube, sie ist unter'm Teppich.
MIAU!

O wohin, wohin,
Ist meine Katze gelaufen?
O wo, o wo kann sie sein?
Mit Ohren so kurz,
Und ihrem Schwanz so lang,
Ich glaube, sie fährt das Auto.
KRACH!

O wohin, wohin,
Ist meine Katze gelaufen?
O wo, o wo kann sie sein?
Mit Ohren so kurz
Und ihrem Schwanz so lang,
Ich glaube, sie ging fort zur See.
AHOI!

O wohin, wohin,
Ist meine Katze gelaufen?
O wo, o wo kann sie sein?
Mit Ohren so kurz,
Und ihrem Schwanz so lang,
O wo, o wo kann sie sein?
MIAU!

Oh where, where
Has my cat gone?
Oh where, oh where can she be?
With ears so short,
And her tail so long,
I think she's up in a tree!
MEOW!

Oh where, where
Has my cat gone?
Oh where, oh where can she be?
With ears so short,
And her tail so long,
I think she's under the rug.
MEOW!

Oh where, where
Has my cat gone?
Oh where, oh where can she be?
With ears so short,
And her tail so long,
I think she's driving the car.
CRASH!

Oh where, where
Has my cat gone?
Oh where, oh where can she be?
With ears so short,
And her tail so long,
I think she went out to sea!
AHOY!

Oh where, where
Has my cat gone?
Oh where, oh where can she be?
With ears so short,
And her tail so long,
Oh where, oh where can she be?
MEOW!

Song to Accompany Story 2

Mein Kätzchen *(My Kitten)*

[Sung to the tune of "The Cat and the Rat" (French Folk Song)]

Mein Kätzchen ist ein hungrige Tier.	*My kitten is a hungry animal.*
Es futtert gern Bananen.	*She likes to eat bananas.*
Es steigt die grünen Bäume rauf	*She climbs up into leafy trees,*
Und frisst sie ganz schnell auf.	*And gobbles them right down.*
Schmatz, schmatz, schmatz, schmatz,	*Munch, munch, munch, munch,*
Es futtert gern Bananen.	*She likes to eat bananas.*
Schmatz, schmatz, schmatz, schmatz,	*Munch, munch, munch, munch,*
Es frisst sie ganz schnell auf.	*She gobbles them right down.*
Mein Kätzchen ist ein hungrige Tier.	*My kitten is a hungry animal.*
Es futtert gerne Äpfel.	*She likes to eat apples.*
Es steigt die grünen Bäume rauf	*She climbs up into leafy trees,*
Und frisst sie ganz schnell auf.	*And gobbles them right down.*
Schmatz, schmatz, schmatz, schmatz,	*Munch, munch, munch, munch,*
Es futtert gerne Äpfel.	*She likes to eat apples.*
Schmatz, schmatz, schmatz, schmatz,	*Munch, munch, munch, munch,*
Es frisst sie ganz schnell auf.	*She gobbles them right down.*
Mein Kätzchen ist ein hungrige Tier.	*My kitten is a hungry animal.*
Es futtert gerne Orangen.	*She likes to eat oranges.*
Es steigt die grünen Bäume rauf	*She climbs up into leafy trees,*
Und frisst sie ganz schnell auf.	*And gobbles them right down.*
Schmatz, schmatz, schmatz, schmatz,	*Munch, munch, munch, munch,*
Es futtert gerne Orangen.	*She likes to eat oranges.*
Schmatz, schmatz, schmatz, schmatz,	*Munch, munch, munch, munch,*
Es frisst sie ganz schnell auf.	*She gobbles them right down.*

Song to Accompany Story 3

Rosa Hunde und blaue Kühe *(Pink Dogs and Blue Cows)*

[Sung to the tune of "My Bonnie Lies over the Ocean"]

Ich dacht' nie, es gäb' rosa Hunde.	*I never believed there were pink dogs.*
Sie sehen so seltsam aus.	*They are such a strange sight to see.*
Ich dacht' nie, es gäb' rosa Hunde,	*I never believed there were pink dogs,*
Doch der da der starrt mich so an.	*But that one is staring at me.*
Wau, wau, wau, wau,	*Ruff, ruff, ruff, ruff,*
Ein rosa Hund starrt mich so an	*A pink dog is staring at me*
—GRAD JETZT!	*—RIGHT NOW!*
Wau, wau, wau, wau,	*Ruff, ruff, ruff, ruff,*
Ein rosa Hund starrt mich so an.	*A pink dog is staring at me.*

Ich dacht' nie, es gäb' blaue Kühe.	I never believed there were blue cows.
Sie sehen so seltsam aus.	They are such a strange sight to see.
Ich dacht' nie, es gäb' blaue Kühe,	I never believed there were blue cows,
Doch die da die starrt mich so an.	But that one is staring at me.

Muh, muh, muh, muh,	Moo, moo, moo, moo,
Eine blaue Kuh starrt mich so an	A blue cow is staring at me
—GRAD JETZT!	—RIGHT NOW!
Muh, muh, muh, muh,	Moo, moo, moo, moo,
Eine blaue Kuh starrt mich so an.	A blue cow is staring at me.

Ich dacht' nie, es gäb' grüne Pferde.	I never believed in green horses.
Sie sehen so seltsam aus.	They are such a strange sight to see.
Ich dacht' nie, es gäb' grüne Pferde,	I never believed in green horses,
Doch das da das starrt mich so an.	But that one is staring at me.

Wieher, wieher,	Neigh, neigh, neigh, neigh,
Ein grünes Pferd starrt mich so an	A green horse is staring at me
—GRAD JETZT!	—RIGHT NOW!
Wieher, wieher,	Neigh, neigh, neigh, neigh,
Ein grünes Pferd starrt mich so an.	A green horse is staring at me.

Song to Accompany Story 4

Tripp tropp *(Drip Drop)*

[Sung to the tune of "Little Bird at My Window" (German Folk Song)]

Tripp tropp. Tripp tropp.	Drip drop. Drip drop.
Tripp tropp. Tripp tropp.	Drip drop. Drip drop.

Komm und schau aus meinem Fenster!	Come and look out my window.
Siehst auch du, was ich seh'?	Do you see what I see?
Ich seh' fünf Regentröpfchen,	I see five little raindrops,
Und sie zwinkern mich an.	Winking back at me.

[*Repeat with* vier Regentröpfchen, *then* drei, *and* zwei Regentröpfchen]	[Repeat with four little raindrops, then three, then two little raindrops.]

Komm und schau aus meinem Fenster!	Come and look out my window.
Siehst auch du, was ich seh'?	Do you see what I see?
Ich seh' ein Regentröpfchen,	I see one little raindrop,
Und es zwinkert mich an.	Winking back at me.

Komm und schau aus meinem Fenster!	Come and look out my window.
Siehst auch du, was ich seh'?	Do you see what I see?
Einen sonnigen Himmel,	A sky full of sunshine,
Und er zwinkert mich an.	Winking back at me.

Komm, wir spielen!	Let's play!

Song to Accompany Story 5

Ich such' *(I'm Looking)*
[Sung to the tune of "Loop-ty Loo"]

Ich such' nach meinem Kätzchen.	*I'm looking for my kitten.*
Ich such' nach meinem Buch.	*I'm looking for my book.*
Ich such' nach meinen Bleistiften.	*I'm looking for my pencils.*
Ich weiß nicht, wo ich suchen soll.	*I don't know where to look.*
Montag, Dienstag, Mittwoch—	*Monday, Tuesday, Wednesday—*
Gleich welchen Tag ich nehm'.	*Any day I choose.*
Donnerstag, Freitag, Samstag,	*Thursday, Friday, Saturday,*
Bis Sonntag verliere ich was.	*By Sunday I lose something.*
Ich such' nach meiner Schildkröte.	*I'm looking for my turtle.*
Ich such' nach meinem Ball.	*I'm looking for my ball.*
Ich such' nach meinen Buntstiften.	*I'm looking for my crayons.*
Ich sehe sie überhaupt nicht.	*I don't see them at all.*
[Repeat chorus.]	[Repeat chorus.]
Ich such' nach meinen Handschuhen.	*I'm looking for my mittens.*
Ich such' nach meinen Schuhen.	*I'm looking for my shoes.*
Ich such' nach meinem Bruder.	*I'm looking for my brother.*
Was kann ich denn sonst noch verliern!	*What else can I lose!*
[Repeat chorus.]	[Repeat chorus.]

Song to Accompany Story 6

Frühling, Sommer, Herbst, Winter
(Spring, Summer, Fall, Winter)
[Sung to the tune of "The More We Get Together" (German Folk Song)]

Ich gab Mutti ein Geschenk,	*I gave Mom a present,*
Ein Geschenk, ein Geschenk.	*A present, a present.*
Ich gab Mutti ein Geschenk,	*I gave Mom a present*
Weil es Frühling war.	*Because it was spring.*
Ich schenkte ihr Blumen,	*I gave her some flowers,*
Gänseblümchen und Rosen.	*Daisies, and roses.*
Ich gab Mutti ein Geschenk,	*I gave Mom a present*
Weil es Frühling war.	*Because it was spring.*
Ich gab Mutti ein Geschenk,	*I gave Mom a present,*
Ein Geschenk, ein Geschenk.	*A present, a present.*
Ich gab Mutti ein Geschenk,	*I gave Mom a present*
Weil es Sommer war.	*Because it was summer.*
Ich schenkte ihr Pfirsiche,	*I gave her some peaches,*
Kirschen und Beeren.	*Cherries, and berries.*
Ich gab Mutti ein Geschenk,	*I gave Mom a present*
Weil es Sommer war.	*Because it was summer.*

Ich gab Mutti ein Geschenk,	I gave Mom a present,
Ein Geschenk, ein Geschenk.	A present, a present.
Ich gab Mutti ein Geschenk,	I gave Mom a present
Weil es Herbst war.	Because it was fall.
Ich schenkte ihr rote Blätter,	I gave her some red leaves,
Grüne und orange Blätter.	Green and orange leaves.
Ich gab Mutti ein Geschenk,	I gave Mom a present
Weil es Herbst war.	Because it was fall.
Ich gab Mutti ein Geschenk,	I gave Mom a present,
Ein Geschenk, ein Geschenk.	A present, a present.
Ich gab Mutti ein Geschenk,	I gave Mom a present
Weil es Winter war.	Because it was winter.
Ich schenkte ihr Schneebälle,	I gave her some snowballs,
Ein paar große, ein paar kleine.	Some big ones, some small ones.
Ich gab Mutti ein Geschenk,	I gave Mom a present.
Weil es Winter war.	Because it was winter.

Song to Accompany Story 7

Eine Katze, zwei Katzen *(One Cat, Two Cats)*
[Sung to the tune of "Where is Thumbkin?"]

Eine Katze, zwei Katzen.	One cat, two cats,
Sieh unsre neue Katze.	See our new cat.
Schau, wie sie spielt.	Watch him play.
So ein schöner Tag!	What a day!
Sie rennt in der Küche rum.	He runs around the kitchen.
Sie rennt im Schlafzimmer rum.	He runs around the bedroom.
O, was für ein Spaß!	Oh, what fun!
Sieh, wie sie rennt!	See him run!
[Repeat chorus.]	[Repeat chorus.]
Sie rennt im Badezimmer rum.	He runs around the bathroom.
Sie rennt im Spielzimmer rum.	He runs around the playroom.
O, was für ein Spaß!	Oh, what fun!
Sieh, wie sie rennt!	See him run!
[Repeat chorus.]	[Repeat chorus.]
Sie rennt in der Stadt herum.	He runs around the city.
Sie sieht so wunderhübsch aus.	He looks so very pretty.
O, was für ein Spaß!	Oh, what fun!
Sieh, wie sie rennt!	See him run!
Sieh, wie sie rennt!	See him run!

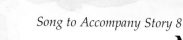

Meine Party *(My Party)*

[Sung to the tune of "El coquí" (Puerto Rican Folk Song)]

Hier sind wir auf der Party,	*Here we are at the party,*
Und so fröhlich, wie man nur sein kann.	*And happy as happy can be.*
Hier sind wir auf der Party,	*Here we are at the party.*
Und alle meine Freunde sind hier.	*And all of my friends are here.*
Hier ist die Katze.	*Here's the cat.*
Sie trägt einen Hut.	*She's wearing a hat.*
Hier sind wir auf der Party,	*Here we are at the party,*
Und so fröhlich, wie man nur sein kann.	*And happy as happy can be.*
Hier sind wir auf der Party,	*Here we are at the party.*
Und alle meine Freunde sind hier.	*And all of my friends are here.*
Hier ist die Schlange.	*Here's the snake.*
Sie frißt noch mehr Kuchen.	*He's eating more cake.*
Da ist die Katze.	*There's the cat.*
Sie trägt einen Hut.	*She's wearing a hat.*
Hier sind wir auf der Party,	*Here we are at the party,*
Und so fröhlich, wie man nur sein kann.	*And happy as happy can be.*
Hier sind wir auf der Party,	*Here we are at the party.*
Und alle meine Freunde sind hier.	*And all of my friends are here.*
Hier ist das Schwein.	*Here's the pig.*
Es tanzt einen Tanz.	*He's dancing a jig.*
Da ist die Schlange.	*There's the snake.*
Sie frißt noch mehr Kuchen.	*He's eating more cake.*
Da ist die Katze.	*There's the cat.*
Sie trägt einen Hut.	*She's wearing a hat.*
Hier sind wir auf der Party,	*Here we are at the party,*
Und so fröhlich, wie man nur sein kann.	*And happy as happy can be.*
Hier sind wir auf der Party,	*Here we are at the party.*
Und alle meine Freunde sind hier.	*And all of my friends are here.*
Hier ist das Pferd.	*Here's the horse.*
Es singt, das ist klar.	*He's singing, of course.*
Da ist das Schwein.	*There's the pig.*
Es tanzt einen Tanz.	*He's dancing a jig.*
Da ist die Schlange.	*There's the snake.*
Sie frißt noch mehr Kuchen.	*He's eating more cake.*
Da ist die Katze.	*There's the cat.*
Sie trägt einen Hut.	*She's wearing a hat.*
Hier sind wir auf der Party,	*Here we are at the party,*
Und so fröhlich, wie man nur sein kann.	*And happy as happy can be.*
Hier sind wir auf der Party,	*Here we are at the party.*
Und alle meine Freunde sind hier.	*And all of my friends are here.*

English/German Picture Dictionary

Here are some of the people, places, and things that appear in this book.

apple
Apfel

bedroom
Schlafzimmer

bakery
Bäckerei

book
Buch

banana
Banane

brother
Bruder

bathroom
Badezimmer

cake
Kuchen

car
Auto

cat
Katze

cows
Kühe

dad
Vati

ears
Ohren

fall
Herbst

fire
Feuer

firehouse
Feuerwehr

fish
Fische

flowers
Blumen

grapes
Trauben

ice cream
Eis

grocery store
Lebensmittelladen

kitchen
Küche

hat
Hut

kitten
Kätzchen

horses
Pferde

leaves
Blätter

hotel
Hotel

library
Bücherei

living room
Wohnzimmer

mom
Mutti

oranges
Orangen

party
Party

people
Leute

pig
Schwein

pond
Teich

post office
Postamt

present
Geschenk

shoes
Schuhen

sister
Schwester

snake
Schlange

snow
Schnee

spring
Frühling

summer
Sommer

tail
Schwanz

town
Stadt

trees
Bäume

turtle
Schildkröte

winter
Winter

Word List

Abenteuer	drei	hallo	liebe	Schlafzimmer	viel
aber	drin	hängen	liebt	Schnee	vielen
acht	drüben	Hans	los	schon	vielleicht
alle	du	Haus	machen	schön	vier
also	Durst	Heim	macht	schwarz	von
am	ein	heißt	mag	Schwester	was
an	eine	helfen	mal	sechs	weiß
anfangen	einen	Herbst	Maria	sehen	wenn
Apfel	einer	herum	meine	sehr	wer
auch	eins	heute	Menge	seht	will
auf	Eis	hier	mich	sein	willst
aus	er	Hilfe	mir	seine	Winter
Bäckerei	erinnert	holen	mit	seinen	wir
Badezimmer	Erinnerungen	Hotel	mitgehen	sich	wissen
Banane	erst	Hunger	Mittwoch	sie	wo
Bäumen	es	hurra	Montag	sieben	Woche
bei	Essen	ich	Morgen	sieht	Wohnzimmer
bekommt	euch	Idee	Mutti	sind	zählt
besser	Familie	ihr	na	so	zehn
Bett	fängt	Ihre	nach	Sommer	Zeit
Bild	fehlt	im	naß	Sonntag	ziehen
Bilder	feiern	immer	nehmen	spielt	zu
bist	Feuer	in	nein	Spielzeug-	zum
bitte	Feuerwehr	ist	neuen	maus	zur
Blätter	finden	ja	neues	Stadt	zwei
Blumen	findet	jetzt	neun	stimmt	
braucht	Fische	kann	nicht	Stunde	
brennt	fragt	Kater	niedlich	Stunden	Durst haben
bringen	Freitag	Kätzchen	niemand	suche	fängt an
Bruder	Frühling	Katze	Nikolaus	suchen	gern machen
Bücherei	fühlen	Katzen	noch	Tag	gib nicht auf
da	fünf	keine	o	Teich	guten
dahin	für	keinen	oder	toll	Morgen
Dank	Futter	klar	orange	tolle	guten Tag
Danke	ganze	klein	Party	trägt	immer noch
Darf	Garten	komm	Postamt	Trauben	in einer
das	gehen	kommt	Prinzessin	trotzdem	Stunde
deine	gern	können	Prinzessinnen	tun	laßt mal
den	gib	könnt	rauf	tut	sehen
denkt	Glück	Küche	raus	überall	sie ziehen los
denn	glücklich	Kuchen	rein	Uhr	macht sich
der	glückliche	lächelt	rosa	um	naß
dich	groß	laßt	ruft	und	schaut mal
die	große	läuft	runter	uns	sieht aus
Dienstag	gut	Lebensmittel-	sagen	Vati	tut mir leid
diese	gute	laden	sagt	verschwun-	ich weiß
dir	guten	leid	Samstag	den	
doch	habe	leider	Schau	verschwun-	
Donnerstag	haben	Leute	schaut	dene	